Madgy Figgy's
Pig

Will Coleman | *Illustrations by Jago Silver*

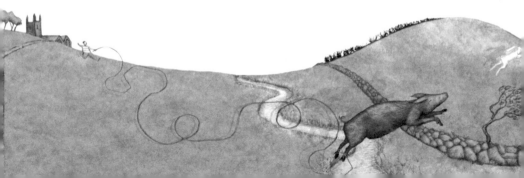

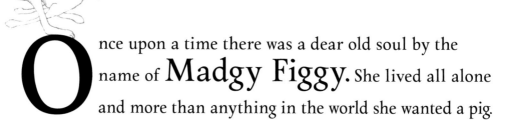

Once upon a time there was a dear old soul by the name of Madgy Figgy. She lived all alone and more than anything in the world she wanted a pig.

She took herself down to the market and had a good look.

Humm...

some of the pigs were too hairy. Some were too thin. Some were too squinty-eyed.

2

But there – in the middle of a great pen of porkers was the perfect pig for Madgy.

Madgy grinned at the pig and gave him a l o n g, s l o w wink. Piggy sat up on his haunches and winked back!

Madgy said, **"Chee-ah, chee-ah!"** which, as you know, is the correct way to call pigs, and the little piggy came trotting over to see her.

She tickled the pig under the chin.
She scratched him behind his floppy earholes.
She ran her finger through his curly tail.

"Piggy," said Madgy, "you and I are going to be
very happy together."

The owner of the pigs came up to Madgy. "Mrs Figgy,
I will sell you that fine pig for five pounds!" he announced.

4

"Bargain!" said Madgy.
"I'll just be off to sell my eggs and butter
and then I'll come back with your money."

But, when she returned to collect her pig, whom should she meet
but her neighbour, Tom Snook, with her piggy under his arm?

"Neighbour Tom!" said Madgy. "I believe that's my pig
you've got under your arm."

"**O**h no it ain't," said Tom. "I paid **six** pounds for that pig. Fair and square I paid that money. My money: my pig. Hard luck, Madgy!"

"Neighbour Tom, I will pay you **seven** pounds for that pig!"

"Huh! No thank you!" said Tom.

"I will pay you **ten** pounds!"

"I don't think so," said Tom. "I won't sell this pig to you, Madgy Figgy, you ole witch. I am going to fatten him up for Christmas time."

"I see," said Madgy Figgy and she leant forward and whispered something into the pig's ear.

"Don't you whisper to my pig!" grunted Tom Snook, snatching him away.

But Madgy just walked off with a mysterious smile.

Tom got home, shoved the pig in the sty and went in for a cup of tea.

No sooner had the cup of tea touched his lips when there was a **knock** at the door –

Knock, knock, knock!

It was his neighbour, Mr Angwyn.

"Tom Snook!" said Mr Angwyn. "Your pig is currently smashing his way through my coldframe and eating my cucumbers!"

"Oh heng!" said Tom. "I best come and sort him out!"

Sure enough, there was the pig, rooting his way through the vegetables and causing no end of destruction.

Well, it took seven or eight men and boys to round Piggy up and get him back into Tom's sty. Tom had to pay for the damage to the coldframe.

This time, Tom made sure the door to the sty was double-bolted and locked and went in for his supper.

But there was another knock on the door.
This time it was his neighbour on
the other side, Mrs Roscrow.

"Tom Snook!" said Mrs Roscrow.

"Your pig is in my begonia bed, munching his way through the flowers!"

"Oh heng!" said Tom. "I best come and sort him out!"

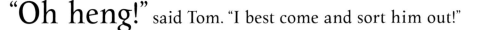

Sure enough, Piggy was out again, destroying Mrs Roscrow's prize flowerbeds.

Once again, it took half the men, boys and girls of Churchtown to round Piggy up and get him back into Tom's sty and, once more, Tom had to pay for the damage.

"Right, we'll keep you in, boy!" said Tom. He put **chicken wire** around the sty. But the pig still got out.

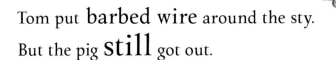

Tom put barbed wire around the sty.
But the pig still got out.

Tom built it up with breeze blocks and an electrified fence.
And Piggy still got out. He was a regular porky Houdini!

Did the pig fatten up? No, he did not.
Whatever Tom tried to feed that pig on, Piggy gobbled it up for
sure, squealed for more, but got no fatter.

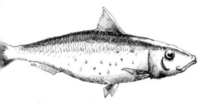

Tom tried him on **bonemeal** and **fishmeal**.
Piggy gobbled it up, squealed for more,
but got thinner and thinner.

Tom tried him on **pasties** and **clotted cream**.

Piggy gobbled it up, squealed for more, but got thinner and thinner.

Tom tried him on **pilchards** and **saffern cake**.

Piggy gobbled it up, squealed for more...

... but got thinner and thinner and thinner.

Soon Tom had had enough of that pig and he wanted rid of him. **"Right,"** he thought, "but I'm not going to sell him to that ole witch Madgy Figgy."

Tom got a nice l o n g bit of string, tied one end of the string around his own wrist, the other end around Piggy's back leg and began to drive the pig to market.

"Gee up, gee up!"

he called and Piggy trotted forward, good as gold.

Everything went very nicely for quite some time.

Suddenly, a great white hare jumped out of the hedge! It sat in the road, right in front of the pig. The pig sat up on his haunches.

The white hare gave the pig a l o n g, s l o w wink and said, "Chee-ah, chee-ah!" Then it was gone, zooming away, over the hedge and up the field.

Piggy took one look at the white hare and fairly flew after it, over the hedge and up the field! Tom's arm was nearly pulled out of its socket. He was j e r k e d across the road and through the hedge.

"Whoa! Stop! Slow down, Piggy! STOP!" shouted Tom.

But it was no good. Piggy wasn't going to stop. The white hare wasn't going to stop. Tom was pulled up the field and down the other side of the hill.

Down at the bottom of the hill where the stream runs under the road there is a drainpipe for the water to run through.

The hare – **vvoooommm!** – shot into the drainpipe under the road.

Piggy – **vvoooommm!** – hurtled in after the hare.

Tom had his arm pulled down into the drainpipe and – **Bam!** – his head slapped up against the side of the road – "**Ow!**"

He gave a pull. "**Erk!**"

But Piggy pulled back. "Oink!"

Tom pulled harder. "Erk! Erk!"

But Piggy pulled back. "Oink! Oink!"

Tom could hardly believe his eyes as he watched the white hare climb out of the other end of the drainpipe and disappear, trotting away through the bushes.

L uckily, Tom had his penknife in   his pocket, and, with his free hand, he managed to get it open, reach inside the drainpipe and cut the string. **What a relief!** He got his arm out of the pipe.

But Piggy was wedged tight, deep down inside the drainpipe.

"Well," thought Tom, "how long can a pig wait? He must be getting hungry.

"After all, it's been a long time since breakfast and if I'm feeling hungry, that pig must be feeling twice as hungry. He will have to come out soon and then I'll grab him!"

Tom sat himself down on the road to wait. The time ticked by and Piggy did not emerge.

Lunchtime came and went. The sun began to get lower over the trees and Piggy stayed put in the drainpipe.

Tom's hunger grew and grew.

Teatime... Suppertime...

Just as he got to thinking about taking off one of his boots and eating that... Who's this trotting down through the wood with her basket over her arm?

Madgy Figgy.

"Neighbour Tom," she said, "what are you doing sitting in the ditch?"

"Pig is in the drainpipe, won't come out and I haven't eaten anything since breakfast!" grunted Tom.

"Oh dear!" said Madgy Figgy. "I don't suppose you would like to sell me the pig now, would you?"

24

"Oh," said Tom. "Sell you the pig, Madgy? Well, I suppose I could let him go for ten pounds."

"Ten pounds, Tom?" said Madgy. "I don't think so."

"No, fair enough, Madgy. How about nine pounds... or eight pounds? I'll tell you what, Madgy, six pounds. That's the price I paid for him.

I'll be getting my money back."

"I don't think so," said Madgy.

"Five pounds?" said Tom. "Four pounds?
Three pounds? Two pounds? One pound?
...Madgy, have you got anything to eat in your basket?"

From her basket, Madgy drew a dry, old crusty end of bread and held it out to Tom.

"Bargain!" said Madgy.

Tom snatched the crust and rammed it into his mouth.

"Right," said Tom. "The pig's in the drainpipe and you'll never get him out!"

And off he stamped, through the wood, shovelling the bread into his mouth, complaining and swearing all the way home.

But Madgy Figgy knelt down by the drainpipe, looked in and gave a l o n g, s l o w wink.

Madgy said, "Chee-ah, chee-ah!" which, as you know, is the correct way to call pigs.

And the little piggy fairly jumped into her arms.

She tickled the pig under the chin.

She scratched him behind his floppy earholes.

She ran her finger through his curly tail.

"Piggy," said Madgy,

"you and I are going to be very happy together."

And they were.

Rag ma whegol Clementine – hoh enwedgack!
For my darling Clementine – a pig in a million!

First published in 2005 by Brave Tales Ltd
This edition published in 2015 by Hope Education
© 2015 Will Coleman
All rights reserved
ISBN 978-1-910605-02-8
Illustrations by Jago Silver
Designed and typeset by Gendall Design
Printed in the UK by Taylor & Clifton Ltd

Hope Education, 2 Gregory Street, Hyde, Cheshire, SK14 4HR
www.hope-education.co.uk

**Other titles in the
Brave Tales series:**

- Tom and the Giant

- Lutey and
  the Mermaid

- Skillywidden

- The Myth of the
  Madron Thorn

- The Ballad
  of Gogmagog

*Free Teacher's Notes are also
available from our website.*